Sex Nymph

By Princess Kink

Table of Contents

Chapter 1: Nymphs

On the edge of the Hardwood Forest, a magical realm was located that the eyes of mere mortals could not so easily penetrate. It was a different world by all means, but it also relied and fed off of the energy that each wanderer brought along with their cautious presence. Tall, muscular warriors with nothing but bear headdresses, leather or cloth pants and boots, were known to lurk within these woods as an initiation ritual of sorts. Their quest was simple: resist temptation and lust throughout the entire twenty-day journey through the forest. Sounds easy, but none so far had been successful.

The twigs snapped underfoot as Halfdan traversed the heavily wooded forest. The air was crisp, and the twittering of birds was prominent. Halfdan was on high alert, knowing full well that these peaceful trees, carrying on as far as the eye could see, were not as peaceful and serene as they seemed. His sword rang as he sliced through the shrubbery, one mighty swing at a time. His tattooed arms flexed with rivers of veins protruding like tunnels of everlasting strength. Halfdan rubbed his white beard with his free hand, trying to get his bearing. All the trees had started to look the same and he saw a pile of severed leaves lying on the ground.

They were the same leaves that he'd sliced only moments ago. He was going in circles.

"Lost, are we?" asked a fair voice. The voice seemed to come from all directions around him, like a tornado of sweet woman's tone.

"Who's there!" growled Halfdan in old Norse.

"I should be asking you that. You're in our woods, Northman. Your gods won't protect you here. We have our own gods who watch over us in these sacred lands…"

"Show yourself!" yelled Halfdan, the leather grip of his sword squeaking with the tension imposed through his hand. She stepped out from between two tall trees, her purple hair longer than her body. She was completely naked, and her body was hairless. The berserker stared at her cleft with lustful eyes. Halfdan adjusted the bear headdress to get a better look. He growled at her like a beast in heat.

"And what is a pretty little thing like you doing out here all on your own, as naked as the day you were born?"

The nymph looked back at him with the darkest brown eyes that he'd ever seen. "You underestimate me, berserker…All those who've underestimated me over the centuries have not lived to tell the tale."

Halfdan sniffed loudly and grasped his trusty sword with both hands, baring his teeth, ready for anything. He had no fear. He never did. Odin was watching him through his one eye. "You're brave and fearless, I'll give you that," said the nymph, her hair spreading around her like the rising sun, creating an entanglement similar to that of a spider's web. Halfdan didn't reply. He didn't waste his time on words with the enemy. Once he'd cast his visual death sentence on someone, it was over.

"Don't…" whispered the gorgeous purple-haired nymph. Halfdan charged her with a deafening growl, letting his sword sink into the edge of her webbed, purple hair. She touched his face and blurred him out of reality, finally able to contain his rage.

Halfdan woke up covered in his brown bear skin. His sword was nowhere to be found, neither was the trusty seax he always carried on his belt. He'd been stripped weaponless and was tied by the wrists with the strongest bonds he'd ever faced. They were the wrappings of the nymph's purple hair. She held him, neutralized and suspended. "Are you done fighting me?"

Halfdan grunted, flexing all of his great muscles to no avail. He nodded at the nymph. "Don't attack me again…I mean it. Next time I will kill you." Halfdan knew that look. It's the same look he'd had in his bloodlust eyes countless times, before the enemy succumbed to the sharp edge of his long blade. "You don't want to fight me. I'm not human."

She let go of Halfdan's wrists with her hair, leaving the confused and disgruntled warrior free with thoughts of defeat and the Allfather. Odin presence wasn't as

—

prominent in the Hardwood Forest. "I won't be overcome by temptation," screamed Halfdan into the sky, like a howling wolf.

The nymph smiled and touched her beautiful, milky body. Her pussy was perfectly pink, like the medium-rare eye of a grilled tenderloin of pork. Halfdan gulped down the salivations that had begun to build up in the back of his throat. His veiny Viking cock was ready to conquer her at any moment. The nymph saw his cock growing underneath his trousers and offered him a wink. She placed her hands on either side of her pussy lips and spread open her vagina. The pink hole was visible from a mile away, tunneling in towards endless, multiple orgasmic pleasures. "You won't be able to resist me…any of us…by the end of today."

That's all she said before walking away towards what looked like a wooden temple. She, as well as dozens of other nymphs, made their way inside the building. Everyone was female and naked inside that place. Halfdan was aroused by the naked bodies inside and his cock began to expel a couple of creamy drops of precum. He groaned a berserker's groan which turned the heads of all the nymphs. He had a very deep voice as it was, and as a grunt it sounded even deeper, as if he were one of Hel's creations. "What is this witchcraft!" he yelled, grinding all the chatter to a halt.

"This is our sanctuary! How dare you speak here you pagan Northman!"

The nymphs all closed in on the lone berserker, well out of his element. Halfdan grabbed the chair next to him and lifted it as if it were a two-handed axe. "You do not want to do that," repeated the purple-haired nymph. She walked towards him with her naked body, twirling her long hair. Her feet slapped the wooden floor. Halfdan looked down and realized that her toes were painted purple, the same color as her hair. Her calves were well-defined and so were her hip bones. More than anything, he noticed her perfect belly button. It looked like a cup of divinity, ready to hold all that was good in this world.

Halfdan gently placed down the chair and stretched the fingers of both his hands, letting the nymphs know that he was no longer a threat. He then got down on one knee, the bear headdress curving over him like a twisted question mark. The purple-haired nymph took his hand and raised him to his feet. "That's better…Now, you can be part of us. We are in need of strong men with cocks the size of Viking longships…"

Halfdan perked up an eyebrow at this left field comment. "My name is Lilla," said the purple-haired nymph with a look of unlocked sex. She walked up to him with slapping footfalls and undid his leather trousers. Halfdan groaned at the sight and sensation of his erect cock being sucked. Lilla knew what she was doing. She offered a few sucks, and then a few licks when the feeling became too overwhelming. Halfdan tried to contain himself. It all felt too good. He was ready to cum ten times over, but his berserker instinct stopped him from indulging, flatlining the sensation as well as the imaginary love.

"No…" he groaned through clenched teeth. "This is the trick which I'm supposed to be resisting." He let out another grunt and then closed his eyes, facing the straw ceiling. His cock started to lose its hardness against all odds. The berserker was tough. He was determined and knew what his mission was on these foreign shores.

The nymphs all looked at him with astonishment. His will was the greatest they'd ever seen. "Submit to us or meet your end!" screamed a nymph with sparkling silver hair. She was the queen of the forest nymphs and held a tall polearm in one hand. Its blade looked like it was made of crystal glass. Halfdan pulled the saliva off his flaccid cock, squeezing out a healthy dose of precum while he was at it, before shoving his package back into his trousers. From within his boot, a compartment which the nymphs had neglected to search, he pulled out a small dagger.

"Valhalla!" he screamed charging the nymph queen with the short but sharp dagger which looked ridiculous, clenched in his large, calloused hand. He was met with a skillful parry that rung around the room. The other nymphs all looked on with shock. They'd never seen a warrior like him before. His sheer determination and fearlessness were enough to make all of their pussies

9

wet. Pussy juice dripped down their inner thighs like sap running down a tree branch.

Their blades danced and whistled through the air, cut after parrying cut. The berserker growled and tackled the nymph queen, slamming her against the floor and spreading her long silver hair across his face in the process. Her scent was exhilarating, and to the nymph queen, the smell of raw man was enough to make her involuntarily spread her legs for him. Halfdan whipped out his dick again and rammed it into the nymph queen, forcing her to sing with ecstasy. The other nymphs were momentarily confused, afraid that their leader had been stabbed by the dagger. They couldn't see well past the bear hide on Halfdan's back, but judging by the pulsing motion of both their hips, they looked and smiled at each other.

Halfdan's big hairy balls clapped against the nymph queen's tight asshole. He suddenly looked up and growled at the ceiling, frothing at the mouth. He groaned at the sensitivity but continued to pump, ensuring that his cum was pushed in as deep as possible through the tunneling walls of her vagina. He suddenly came to his senses and ripped his cock out of her, violently stuffing it back into his trousers. What had he done? He'd failed the test! He'd succumbed to the seduction of these treacherous forest nymphs. "What is your name, mighty Northman?" asked the nymph queen, looking up at him from the floor with seductive eyes.

"Halfdan."

"I'll make sure that our son will carry his father's name for as long as he shall live. He'll be destined to do great things. Things that no Northman has ever done before."

"Son? What are you talking about woman!" snapped Halfdan, more angry with himself than anyone else for being so weak.

"You have put a son in my belly. He grows, even now."

The door slammed against the wall loudly behind them, turning the heads of all the nymphs and the lone berserker, who was clearly out of his element. It was Lilla. She'd slammed the door open against the wall and had stormed out, her beautiful purple hair flowing behind her and on the ground. She seemed to be holding her face with both hands. Whispers broke out between the other nymphs around the room, and Halfdan looked down at the nymph queen, offering her his hand. She took it and the berserker pulled her up to her feet. She wore sandals made of green ivy that curled around and between each of her pristine toes.

"What happens now?" asked Halfdan, sensing the eyes peering at him through his headdress.

"Now, you may continue on your journey…but be warned. There are older and more terrible dangers out there than us peaceful forest nymphs."

Halfdan raised his eyebrow in disbelief. They were just going to let him go? "What about this son, growing in your belly?"

"He's my son. We will raise him and prepare him for the world. You do not need to do anything. He'll come looking for you someday. We'll teach him all about Halfdan the Fearless…" One of the nymphs brought Halfdan his sword, seax, and the sharpening stone he always carried in his pocket. He sheathed his sword and seax and looked around the nymphs' camp. It was tranquil here, far too tranquil for a berserker seeking the gory details of his yet to be saga. Halfdan sniffed the air and walked away, making his way deep into the forest again. Lilla looked on with teary eyes as the bear headdress slowly disappeared from sight.

Chapter 2: Dwarves

Halfdan continued to cut and slice his way through the darkening woods. He couldn't tell if the darkness was caused by the day turning to night, or if the thick foliage was blocking out the sun. His stomach grumbled loudly. He hadn't eaten for at least a day, and with muscles like that, he needed to eat at least five times a day, especially if he'd ejaculated a hefty load on top of that.

He saw the stag in the distance, popping its mighty antlers up into the air as a sign of dominance. Halfdan backed off and severed a long branch from the healthiest looking tree. He sharpened the branch with his sword into a spear. He worked quickly and quietly as to not scare off or lose track of the juicy stag. Right as he took aim with a steady hand and was about to fling the spear with precision, firm fingers wrapped themselves around his bulging bicep. He turned around and tackled the mystery guest, pointing the sharp end of the spear at her fearful eyes. It was Lilla.

"What are you doing here!" he whispered through clenched teeth. Once he was in kill mode, it was hard to undo the buildup of rage.

"I came to warn you. Any lives that you take in these woods will be met with dire consequences. All the

---

animals and creatures here are protected by our gods. They do not take kindly to outsiders…especially outsides who kill our majestic creatures."

Halfdan looked over his shoulder after hearing the galloping sound of receding hooves. The stag was gone. "See what you did! What am I supposed to eat on my journey through this never-ending forest?"

Lilla pushed Halfdan aside and slowly stood up. The side of his bearded face brushed past her silky hips. She turned herself at the last second, ensuring that the Viking's big nose was hooked between her pussy lips, just long enough for him to catch a strong whiff of the honey-like juices tumbling within her sweet walls. He shook with lust and stuck his tongue out, licking nothing but air. Lilla laughed and pushed him off. Halfdan growled. He didn't like to be teased, especially by purple-haired and purple-toenailed, naked nymphs.

"There is another way," said Lilla, sensing his anger brewing to uncontrollable limits. "Another way for you to get fed…"

"And what is that?"

"Me. The fluids that I excrete are more than enough to sustain any mortal. In fact, they are so pure that they do more than just sustain…they are the building blocks for life to thrive."

Halfdan's jaw dropped at the proposition. "What fluids are you talking about exactly? You want me to eat your piss and shit?"

"No, warrior. Unless that's your thing? Any fluids will suffice, from my sweat to my tears, to other fluids…"

Halfdan looked down at her bare, spotless pussy. His mouth began to water again. "Why are you doing this? What's in it for you?"

"I need you to kill the mountain trolls who've been plaguing these lands. They don't take us nymphs seriously. They belong to your gods, not ours. They've been invading…penetrating our peaceful borders deeper and deeper, with no fear or challenge."

"Mountain trolls? I'm a lone berserker…I'm not equipped to take on a whole tribe of mountain trolls by myself, that would be suicide."

Lilla's hair twirled up into the air by itself before wrapping around her bare body like the tobacco leaves of a cigar. "You won't be alone. First, we'll need to assemble an army of our own…but before we even think about that, I need you to be fed and at peak strength." She curled her index fingers at him. Halfdan stepped forward and her beautiful purple hair made an opening for him, right by her slit. She was telling him where she would like him to get his feed from this time around.

Halfdan pulled his bear headdress down his back a bit and kneeled in front of her glorious pussy. "Rub it and lop up as much of my wetness as you'd like…to your heart's content." Halfdan offered her swollen little clit a lick. It replied by hardening and filling with beautiful nymph's blood. He'd never licked a vagina like this before. Normally, they were hairy, and even the women who took extra care shaving…they would still be inevitably prickly. Lilla had absolutely no body hair and therefore, had never had the need to shave. Licking a completely smooth, barren, warm body flowing with the juices of live was something else entirely.

She tasted so good and so pure that Halfdan almost came in his trousers. Lilla's moan was the sweetest moan he'd ever heard. Her facial expressions and bodily movements showed him that she was close to cumming. She grabbed the bear headdress by the ears and then moved down towards Halfdan's bald, tattooed head. She ran her fingers along old tattoos of Fenrir and Týr, in between lines of battle scars. She pushed his head hard against her clit and then let out a squeal which echoed around the forest, as she squirted into his mouth, invigorating him instantly.

To his surprise, Halfdan was full and felt better than he'd ever felt before. He inhaled the fresh forest air, ready for a fight in the name of the Allfather! "Let's go. My blade aches for the taste of fresh, warm blood!" he growled, peering through the thicket. Lilla, her body covered in beads of sweat, nodded and led the way southeast.

"Our first stop, the dwarves. Be warned, they do not like company…especially company who are taller than they are."

Halfdan looked over at Lilla with a puzzled looked. "I thought you said that my gods do not exist here. Dwarves? They are part of us Northmen."

"These aren't like any dwarves you've ever met," laughed Lilla. They continued their journey over the hills and through many a copse, until they came upon a stonewalled enclosure.

"Who are 'ye, and why 'ave 'ye come to our lands!" yelled a short man wrapped in a silk cloak. Halfdan looked at him and then at Lilla.

"I would've preferred our kind of hammer wielding dwarf…" he whispered to her.

"Would 'ye now? Well, 'ye are more than welcome to fuck 'yer way off out of 'ere!"

Halfdan didn't realize that this breed of forest dwarf had excellent hearing, unlike the counterpart he was used to in the Northland.

"He means no harm. He's here to help us. Wouldn't you want to free yourselves from the constant pestering of those stinky mountain trolls?" said Lilla, stepping in front of Halfdan. The dwarf contemplated what she said for a moment. He then looked up and nodded at her.

"Keep a leash on 'yer warrior over 'der, I don't like the looks of 'im. Looks like he's into bestiality or something…"

Halfdan began unsheathing his sword with bared teeth at this comment, but Lilla stopped him and gave him a look of reprimand. "Follow me!" yelled the dwarf, opening the tiny gate to their enclosed village. Halfdan was instantly the center of attention. Little silk covered dwarves stared at him with jaws ajar. He pulled his headdress over his head, which got him even more attention. His headdress was caked in dried blood from previous combat. Only the rain had ever washed it, and even that was not enough to get out all the gore and historical filth.

"What do these dwarves do here all day?" asked Halfdan, looking around the barren community. There was hut after hut with what looked like a great hall in the center. Halfdan raised an eyebrow at the passionate sounds coming from within the great hall. Their dwarf guide opened the doors and Halfdan almost burst out into laughter at the sight. Dozens of dwarves, male and female, were tangled in a web of orgies. Their high-pitched voices sounded like fingernails on a chalkboard.

"Does that answer your question?" whispered Lilla sarcastically, shaking her head.

"And who might you be!" boomed a red-bearded dwarf, something closer to what Halfdan imagined dwarves would look like, though he was still wearing a silk cloak. His stubby chode was out with strings of precum dragging across the floor. "Bring me that cute little ass of yours!" yelled the red-bearded dwarf, who seemed to be the leader of this peculiar village. Halfdan looked at Lilla, who was covering her body with her purple hair. She looked back at him and grinned.

"He's talking to you, not me," she laughed. Halfdan's eyes grew to the size of dinner plates.

"Yes, you! The bear! Come over here and take my load deep in that virile, chiseled asshole of yours!"

Halfdan placed his hand on the handle of his sword again, which the dwarf guide who'd let them in immediately picked up on.

"Sire! I don' think he's into that! He's a warrior from distant lands, come to 'elp us!"

"I need to cum!" howled the dwarf lord, violently jerking off his beer can of a cock. He shot his load past Halfdan's face, almost catching him in the eye. The berserker finally lost it. He pulled his sword out with a stout ring and growled his way in milliseconds towards the dwarf lord, who hadn't come back to his senses yet, still clinging onto his sensitive cockhead. Halfdan placed him in a headlock and dug the sharp edge of the sword hard against his throat, drawing a few drops of blood. His tattooed muscles glistened in the light of the fire from the center of the room.

"Don't!" screamed Lilla. "Please, they are our friends! They're just a bit…oversexed and love to engage in never-ending orgies."

Halfdan looked down in horror to see the dwarf lord shaking profusely. He was still masturbating, using his own slippery cum as lube. He was torturing his own cockhead by rubbing it to beyond sensitive lengths. Halfdan let go of him and kicked him in his back, sending the dwarf flying across the room, barely missing the fire by mere inches. "What kind of army is this! Fucking like rats in the shadowy corners of this disgusting room! I could butcher everyone here in less than a minute!"

"I don't doubt your strength," said the dwarf lord, grabbing his ass and grinning from the floor. He was still on all fours and started to laugh. "That was a good kick!" He then got up and arched his back, his semi-erect cock dripping the remnants of cum all over the ground. The other dwarves around him were still fucking and sucking each other off. Halfdan let out a grunt of disapproval when he saw that they had no care whatsoever what or whom their cocks ended up in. It was a free for all fuck buffet. Dwarf man on dwarf man, dwarf man on dwarf woman, dwarf woman on dwarf woman…there was even a goat bleating, somewhere inside the perverse fuckfest. "Lilla! Didn't see you there love, how've you been?" asked the dwarf lord, finally putting his cock back inside his patchy pants.

"Hello Lord Redbeard. You must forgive us. We mean you and your village no harm. On the contrary, I've brought this berserker here to crush our enemies, so that everything can go back to normal without the constant pestering of mountain trolls!"

"How many warriors do you need?" asked Lord Redbeard, speaking loudly over the goat which seemed to be cumming? Halfdan shuddered at the thought. He couldn't see the goat, buried beneath the piles of heavy breathing, naked, sweaty bodies…but he didn't need to in order to know that something was definitely wrong.

"As many as you can spare. Mountain trolls are tall and powerful. They're easily confused by numbers. The more warriors we have spread out around them, the more confused and sluggish they'll become."

"What are you gonna do…fuck 'em to death?" asked Halfdan, sliding his sword through the boar roasting over the open fire. He prayed to Freya that the glistening animal on the spit didn't have a surprise cream filling…

The sliver of meat he cut off was cooked and steaming. He took a bite then looked around the room. There was ale and mead stored in large wooden barrels. He grabbed the drinking horn on his belt and opened the lid of the nearest barrel. He then dunked his horn in, filling it to the brim, before chugging down the ale with loud slurps. The ale soaked his chest, using his beard as its swift highway. The berserker belched loudly and filled his horn again, and a third time. He kept going until he laughed with tipsy giddiness. "Fuck it! Let's attack the mountain trolls with a bunch of horny dwarves. Just please, bring a weapon that isn't your cock!"

Lilla let out an uncomfortable laugh and Lord Redbeard slapped his knee with glee. "Then it is settled! I will make sure that my warriors are ready and prepared for battle by tomorrow morning. Let's hunt some mountain troll!" The berserker yelled into the ceiling before plunging his sword into the side of the ale barrel, and placing himself right beneath the heavy, piss-like stream.

Chapter 3: Sexy Feet

Halfdan woke up the next morning, his face sticky with ale. He felt something warm touch his cheek, digging through his clumped-up beard to get to the skin. "Wake up sleepy head," said Lilla with a fair voice. He opened his blue eyes and realized that she was touching him with her salty toes. They were a bit damp and had a slight smell that reminded him of fresh cheese mixed with the scent of an earthy cave.

"Mmm," groaned the berserker, grabbing his forehead. He'd drank a bit too much as he always did when there was an abundance of ale.

"Have a snack," said Lilla, shoving her toes into his mouth before he could respond and grabbing his tongue. Halfdan scrunched his face at the overwhelming sourness. He was about to complain, but realized that her sweat, even if it had come from between her stinky toes, had invigorated him, completely curing his hangover.

"You can have the other foot later if you'd like," said Lilla with a pronounced wink. "How are we looking?" she then said, turning towards Lord Redbeard. Behind the dwarf lord stood an army of fourteen or so warriors, if you could call them that. They carried swords which were closer to large daggers in size, and they all wore red silk shirts, which wouldn't stop even a glancing blow from cutting the man wearing it.

"Thómas, I leave you in charge while we go hunting for some mountain trolls! Take good care of my halls and village," said Lord Redbeard, fastening his own golden dagger-like sword around his waist. Thómas turned out to be the name of the dwarf who'd let Halfdan and Lilla through the main gate.

"Very good, sire!" he boomed back.

Halfdan blew on the ram's horn attached to his belt, striking fear into the heart of everyone within a two-mile radius. They were off, wandering through the forest towards the snowy mountains to the north. After marching for about three hours, they stopped to make camp. There was no food to be found and Halfdan looked over to Lilla. "What are the dwarves going to eat?" asked Halfdan, already fearing the answer to his question.

"Each other," replied Lilla, covering her mouth with her hand to stop herself from blatantly laughing at the increasingly uncomfortable berserker. The dwarves had already started fondling each other, sucking on cocks and a variety of body parts. "This forest is ruled over by the goddess of sex. She feeds us through lust. You're lucky that you have me by your side. Nymphs are by far the most nutritious…" She took Halfdan by his calloused hand and led him away from camp. "I want to be fed too," she whispered in his ear, offering his earlobe a small lick. Her long hair parted and pulled Halfdan in close.

The berserker stripped off all of his clothes, leaving him bare-assed and tattooed for all the gods, foreign or native, to see. Lilla ran her fingers over the many scars, products from a lifetime of war and sword cuts. She touched the small craters on his chest, remnants of arrowhead wounds. With her other hand, she fondled his large, low-hanging balls. Halfdan moaned, growing rapidly in size. He kissed her on the mouth, sucking on her pink tongue. Her saliva tasted fresh and clean, like a rejuvenating waterfall deep from within the mountains. He bottled her spit at the source and swallowed it. He then stuck his tongue out and licked her neck, moving down towards her beautiful breasts. He moistened her nipples before blowing on them. They saluted him like two perfectly shaped bullets. He sucked on them as Lilla let out a loud moan. She loved having her nipples touched. Her pussy had started to drip, and with no hair to get in its way, gravity was easily able to pull down her clear, sticky juices, running down her legs all the way to her knees. Halfdan looked at the sticky trail of sex juices. They'd moved past her knees and around her curvy calves and down her ankles, towards her feet.

Halfdan kneeled down and picked up her right foot and sucked the pussy juices out from between her toes. His eyes rolled back into his head at the savory sweet flavor ruling his palate. Her foot sweat had mixed with the sweet honey from her vagina, creating a perfect balance of flavors. After he'd sucked her toes clean and licked the dirt covered bottoms of her sole, he moved onto the left foot and gave it the exact same treatment. He then licked all the way up her long leg. Lilla let out a loud feminine moan as the berserker reached her pussy. He parted her lips with his tongue and lopped up the remaining honey straight from the hive.

Lilla pulled Halfdan up to his feet and bent over for him. Her sugar walls opened up like Valhalla's gates, with sticky strings between them. The berserker pulled back the foreskin from his fat cockhead before shoving his astonishing length deep inside her warmth. "Don't cum in me," she said. Halfdan wasn't sure if he could keep this promise, but he nodded anyway, stupidly realizing that she couldn't see him with her back turned to him. It'd been a while since he'd fucked a woman as smooth and fair as she was. Most of the Viking women back home were covered in tattoos. He'd forgotten what spotless beauty looked like on the canvas of a curvy, feminine body.

He pounded her tight little cunt as if Ragnarök itself had been initiated. She screamed into her purple hair, unable to keep the burning passion bottled up any longer. She'd never had Viking cock before and Halfdan's navigation of his manhood was long-lived and true. The berserker started to pant loudly, letting Lilla know that he was on the verge of cumming. She quickly pushed him off and dropped to her knees, cupping her lips around his blood stuffed erection. He came rivers into her mouth, which she drank as if it were the thick, white smoothie of life itself. His cockhead was so swollen that it didn't allow his foreskin to retract in order to shield his sensitivity. Halfdan groaned as if he'd taken an arrow to the chest again. He didn't mind getting cut, stabbed, or shot by arrows or crossbow bolts. For some reason, the sensitivity of his cockhead was the worst of all, enough to bring the big grizzly berserker to his knees like a little schoolboy.

"Ahh!" he howled out of tune. Lilla looked up at him and giggled. She grabbed the base of his cock and moved her hand up, squeezing out every last drop of Viking babies. He jerked and twitched through the unbearable sensitivity, until she finally let go of him and pushed him out of her throat. She pulled his foreskin back over his cockhead on his behalf.

"Wouldn't want him to get cold, it's almost nightfall." She stood back up and untangled her hair. Halfdan looked around and immediately blushed with embarrassment. The dwarves were standing around them in a circle whooping and clapping at the bare-assed berserker and forest nymph. Halfdan quickly got dressed and pulled his headdress over his head as low as it could go.

"Sorry lad! We meant no harm with our intrusion. We thought that you may have landed yourself in some kind of trouble. That orgasmic howl you let out was loud and desperate enough to attract both man, beast, and everything in between!" said Lord Redbeard. The rest of the dwarves laughed. Most of them still had their stubby dicks out, dripping with the remnants of cum guzzling orgasms. Their lips and beards were also white, confirming the act and result.

"Now that we're all fed, let's discuss our game plan," said Lilla, trying her best to break the awkward silence. Halfdan cleared his throat and looked around the circle jerk of half flaccid dwarves.

"Well? Care to share with me what your dwarven battle tactics are, Lord Redbeard?" asked Halfdan with a strong hint of sarcasm. It was more than a hint really, more like a gleaming north star of sarcasm.

"Do you not think that we are capable of war?" asked Lord Redbeard, offended for the first time. He'd let Halfdan kick him across his great hall, but it was this blatant display of disrespectful sarcasm that'd finally sent the dwarf lord over the edge.

"Why don't you convince me otherwise then?" replied Halfdan, pulling his headdress back up a bit so that the dwarves could see his bloodshot berserker's eyes. Lord Redbeard gestured for all of them to return back to the campfire. It was getting dark and creatures could be heard growling and howling into the darkening skies. He grabbed a stick and kicked the leaves on the forest floor aside, leaving behind only the dirt and sand. In it, he drew five large, hunched over figures.

"Let's pretend that these are mountain trolls. What we need to do is spread out around them as far as possible, while still looking like a single unit. We then stab them from all sides and hope that we can dodge their big clubs in time, before one of us gets clobbered over the head!"

Halfdan looked back unimpressed. "What're you going to stab them with? Those toothpicks you carry on your waists?" he laughed.

"These toothpicks as you call them, are some of the sharpest blades in the entire world. They'll slip through the hardest and toughest armor like a hot poker going through butter. Trust me, they are more than enough to get the job done."

"We believe you, Lord Redbeard," answered Lilla, giving Halfdan a look of disapproval.

"Yes, Lord Redbeard," Halfdan added in. "I'm sure that stabbing their toes with sharp pokers will topple over these mighty mountain trolls. If you don't mind, I'll be in charge of the battle plan."

"Have you ever fought a mountain troll before!" boomed Lord Redbeard, getting up to his feet. He was ready to challenge the insolent berserker.

"No."

"Then why would you be in charge of the battle plan?"

"We'll do it your way Lord Redbeard, thank you. Halfdan and I are tired from all the endless marching. Goodnight!" interjected Lilla, before Halfdan could make things worse. She grabbed him firmly by the wrist with her superhuman strength and walked a few paced towards the edge of camp. Her hair immediately curled around both of their bodies again, taking the shape of a roomy tent.

"I don't need you to fight my battles for me, nymph!" growled Halfdan, ready to draw his sword and cut through her magical hair if he needed to, in order to get to Lord Redbeard. She instantly neutralized him by grabbing his cock from behind.

"Lie down on me and face the night sky," she whispered into his ear, instantly calming him down and redirecting his remaining anger towards his mighty erection. Halfdan lay down on her with his back against her pubic bone. She kissed his neck and wrapped her legs around his waist and thighs. She dug into the sides of his knees with the arches of her feet and pushed his legs apart. Her hands went exploring inside his pants, unleashing his long, veiny cock. She cupped her arches together around his cock and began to give him a slow and forceful footjob. The berserker grunted as his loins began to sing and tremble with excitement.

Lilla curled her perfectly straight, purple toes up so that Halfdan could get a closer look. "Do you like the color?" she moaned into his ear. Halfdan nodded, the bear headdress jiggling on top of his skull. "Good. I'm stuck with the color. All forest nymphs have colored toenails that match their hair color, but that rule only applies to our toenails. Our fingernails are barren, so let me know if you'd like me to paint them a color of your choosing."

Halfdan didn't care. He was enjoying the footjob with closed eyes. Her sexy, smooth calves pressed hard against his scarred abs and tattooed sides. He grabbed her ankles and moved her feet up and down faster, getting ready for the climax. It came right as Lilla had started to pinch his nipples and nibble on his ears. He shot his creamy seed high into the air. Lilla maneuvered her feet in such a way, that not even a drop of sperm was wasted. She caught it all on the top of her foot, toes, and soles. She brought her own feet to her mouth with incredible flexibility and licked and slurped every last drop, ensuring that she was good and fed for the night. Halfdan placed his head back between her bosom and started to snore loudly. She smiled and hugged her grizzly man, closing her gorgeous eyes, so that they would comfortably sleep in each other's arms peacefully through the cold night.

Chapter 4: Mountain Trolls

Their sleep was cut short. Everyone was awoken by a succession of loud smashing sounds. "What the fuck is going on!" yelled Halfdan. Lilla instantly covered his mouth.

"Quiet! We're hidden out of sight as long as we stay inside the shroud of my hair. The same rules don't apply to sound, they can still hear us, so shut up!" she hissed into his ear. She tightened her legs and feet around his body to stop him from getting up and doing something stupid, like getting himself killed.

"But…the dwarves…What is out there?" Halfdan mumbled through the covered palm of Lilla's hand. The dwarves could be heard screaming and grunting not too far away, by the dying remnants of the once blazing campfire. A horrible stench suddenly made its way through the thick strands of purple hair. A low rumbling growl, like the kind made by dire beasts, shook everything around them.

"Mountain trolls…They must've caught our scent," said Lilla. Halfdan pushed her legs and feet aside with his powerful hands. He then tucked his flaccid cock back into his trousers and unsheathed his sword. "What're you going to do? Mountain trolls never travel alone. They'll crush you!"

The berserker wasn't listening. From his belt, he pulled open the strings of a small leather pouch. "What is that?" asked Lilla, looking at the dried bits of what looked like boiled shoe leather.

"Mushrooms," replied Halfdan, taking a small handful and popping them into his mouth. He chewed them profusely and swallowed them with a few gulps, as they were very dry and clung to his throat. He started to cough, and his face turned blue. A few pieces had gotten stuck on their way down. Lilla instantly placed her pussy against his discolored lips and pressed him hard against her. A steady stream of piss was more than enough to dislodge the dried bits of mushroom. Forest nymph piss had the added bonus of decreasing the time it took for such a substance to take effect. Halfdan was pleasantly surprised at the flavor as well. Her warm piss tasted like thyme infused herbal tea.

He smiled up at her as the stream cut off. She noticed the white froth pooling around the sides of his lips, dripping down onto his thick beard. Halfdan's body started going into convulsions. She couldn't tell if he was cumming or if something else was going on. The frothing berserker suddenly pulled himself up to his feet. His eyes were bloodshot beyond belief and he looked truly scary. Lilla pulled her hair back, allowing the berserker to focus on someone or something else to attack.

Five towering mountain trolls with greyish white fur that reeked of fetor were smashing the trees in an attempt to catch an unsuspecting dwarf on the head. It looked like a bad game of Whac-A-Mole. Halfdan instantly sprang into action, slicing open the nearest troll's shin. Dark red, almost black blood oozed out, bathing everyone below the troll in iron rich gore. Before the wounded troll had a chance to react, Halfdan had sliced open his other shin, toppling over the great mountain troll. Its greyish white fur was now blood red and glistened in the moonlight.

Halfdan grabbed Lord Redbeard off the ground. The dwarf lord was cowering with his head dug deep into the dirt like an ostrich hiding from a chasing lioness. "Show me how sharp that sword is. Skewer that motherfucker straight through the ankles!" shouted Halfdan, pointing at the second mountain troll with the tip of his bloodied sword. Lord Redbeard panted and charged with his eyes closed at the second troll. He wasn't lying. His toothpick sword was indeed very sharp, which he proved by running the nearest tree clean through. Even the mountain troll looked down at him confused. "Fucking idiot!" muttered Halfdan beneath his quivering breath. He shook with rage and invisibility. He threw his sword as hard as he could at the troll, right before the troll's own clubbed swing was about to flatten Lord Redbeard.

The troll's club barely nicked Lord Redbeard's thigh, which in turn caused him to develop the largest erection any dwarf had ever developed in these distant lands.

Lord Redbeard groaned as his cock started to swell beyond its limit. He needed to jack off in order to save his own life. He went to work, moving up and down his chode with so much velocity, that it looked like it was about to catch on fire. He ejaculated rope after rope of heavy, double-double dwarf cream. A scream unlike any that Halfdan or any of them had ever heard before cut through the night, ringing in their ears like an erupting volcano. The mountain troll's skin had started to sizzle. The dwarf's cum turned out to be lethal, melting away patches of fur and skin as if it were acid.

Lord Redbeard looked at his warriors and felt useful for the first time in his life. "Spray 'em down, boys!" he commanded, raising his fist into the air. The dwarves all dropped their weapons and slid off their trousers. Bare-assed and panting, the dwarf soldiers began to suck each other off, while doing their best to dodge the whooshing swings from the remaining trolls' clubs. The night was suddenly plagued by the sounds of high-pitched moans and spit covered cocks being handled with mastery. Airborne jizz found its target, over and over again. The trolls continued to shriek as their skin sizzled. Halfdan dodged the ropes with great agility and retrieved his sword before it was drenched in dwarf cum. They looked like pigeons splattering their white load all over the town square.

A woman's scream cut through the crisp air like a stiff dagger. Halfdan turned around to see the last mountain troll making a run for it. It had Lilla wedged in its powerful grip, carrying her off like King Kong to some remote cave, high up in the frozen mountains. "No!" yelled Halfdan, running after them. Right as he was about to catch up to the escaping mountain troll, Halfdan was knocked off his feet. The mountain trolls' combined shrieking and the sounds of battle had attracted all sorts of creatures and beasts to their position. Skeletal soldiers with rusted chainmail were staring back at Halfdan.

"What is this witchcraft?" he mumbled to himself. Lord Redbeard had joined him by his side after retrieving his toothpick sword from the nearby tree, which he'd kebabbed.

"They are the fallen soldiers of these woods. Many of them are Northmen like you," said the dwarf lord with a gulp.

"Put your cock away before I chop it off," said Halfdan without changing his gaze, fixated on the numerous undead piling up in front of him like a reanimated graveyard. Lord Redbeard obeyed, squeezing out the remaining few drops which his cock hadn't been able to pump out in the heat of the moment. "Tell your warriors to create a shield wall behind me."

Lord Redbeard turned his head and signaled the rest of the dwarves to come over. They'd successfully brought down four out of the five mountain trolls to their knees with sheer cum. "I'm not gonna repeat it again…everyone put your cocks away! Cum isn't going to save us against this boneyard…Shield wall!"

"But…we have no shields…" said one of the warriors.

"Just line up and draw your swords. Hit them hard! Swing…don't stab. Stabbing a skeleton isn't going to do anything. Ready? Charge!" Halfdan downed another quick mouthful of shrooms as the dwarves charged the advancing skeleton army. Halfdan then took out his horn and blew on it, invigorating the silk and sperm covered dwarves. He swung his sword hard and true, snapping the first skeletal warrior and his corroded chainmail in half. The dwarves did not heed his advice and lost their swords in a matter of seconds, getting the guards stuck in ribcages and other crevices. Not knowing what else to do, they whipped their cocks back out and started to jack off profusely.

The skeletal warriors were so confused by this act that they all stopped fighting and looked back through decomposed eye sockets at the dripping dwarves. This gave Halfdan the perfect opportunity to cleave through the enemy, severing bone limbs and heads, rendering the undead utterly useless. After they were defeated, Halfdan averted his eyes and plugged his ears with both thumbs. He didn't want to hear or see the orgasmic dwarves, shooting what was left inside their big, church bell balls.

"Lilla!" yelled the berserker at the top of his lungs. The forest had now grown silent as the many simultaneous climaxes came to an end. Lilla and the mountain troll who took her were nowhere to be seen. Halfdan ran through the forest as fast as he could in the direction he'd last seen Lilla being dragged off to. Lord Redbeard yelled something after the sprinting berserker, but Halfdan's legs carried him so fast that he couldn't quite make out what he'd said. Very soon he was alone in the silent forest with nothing but his own panting breath to keep him company. He wasn't sure if he was going the right way or if he'd missed a turn somewhere. The leaves were wide and thick, disallowing the guiding stars from showing him the way.

Halfdan ran like this for a few hours, until the first rays of light dawned the morning. The mountain trolls' blood had hardened across his tattooed chest and on his sword. The northern mountains could be seen far away in the distance and looked too difficult to climb for a lone warrior lost within the forest of foreign gods. "Odin! Fill me with strength and guide me to Lilla! Let there be no deception or trickery!" Halfdan screamed into the cold air. His breath came out like a spewing geyser, reminding the berserker of how cold it really was. He tightened his headdress across his broad shoulders and knew that the only way to retain heat was to keep on moving. His feet ached and his legs were cramping up, but there was no time. He needed to save his love from the horrible fate awaiting her, deep within the stinky mountain troll caves, hollowed out for one purpose: to skewer and eat all the fair creatures of the Hardwood Forest. Mountain trolls were hunter gatherers, and fair creatures who are pure of heart, such as nymphs, were highly prized possessions. They also tasted the best.

Halfdan sniffed the air. He could smell meat being roasted over an open fire. His heart suddenly dropped. Was he too late? He rushed through the thicket and over a small hill covered in frosted rime. Smoke was bellowing into the air in great quantities. There was a fire alright. Halfdan squinted and saw a peculiar figure hunched over next to a twisted tree. A raven flew by his head and landed on top of a nearby branch. It peered through Halfdan's soul, as if the Allfather himself were present in this moment. Aren't you gonna join me? He heard a decrepit old man's voice ringing through his mind. It'd come from the peculiar figure, who was now covered in smoke. He was burning something. Something that smelled like divine flesh, not fit for the torturous fate of flames. Halfdan's mind wandered and he grasped his sword with white knuckles, before walking over to the hunched over man covered in smoke, ready to provide his swift punishment. Halfdan raised his sword, ready to strike the old man. His arm froze midair and a twisted, jaw dropping expression inhabited his face. He couldn't believe what the old man was roasting over the fire…